For my fabulous nieces and nephew—
Ramie, Emma, Tillie, Hannah, Mimi and Louis.
Lots of love!
Aunt Laurie
—L.B.F.

For Elliot and Juliette, who are both
exceptionally creative and artistic
—J.K.

High Five, Mallory!

by Laurie Friedman

illustrations by Jennifer Kalis

darbycreek

MINNEAPOLIS

CONTENTS

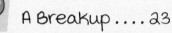
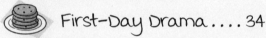

A WORD FROM MALLORY

My name is Mallory McDonald, like the restaurant, but no relation. I'm ten years old and I had the most action-packed summer of my life!

I planted a garden (FUN!) with my neighbor. I took an art class. (SUPER FUN!) I went on a trip with my family to the Grand Canyon. (SUPER DUPER FUN!) And I helped my best friends, Mary Ann and Joey, move to a new house across town. (Not so much fun, because I was sad they wouldn't be living next door to me anymore!)

Now, it's back-to-school time in Fern Falls. Come Monday morning, Mary Ann, Joey, Chloe Jennifer, and I will be starting 5th grade at Fern Falls Elementary. My brother, Max, and his girlfriend, Winnie, who also happens to be Joey's sister and Mary Ann's stepsister, are heading to 7th grade at Fern Falls middle School.

This is the first year max and I won't be at the same school. It's too bad—we got along better than ever this summer, even though we still argued sometimes. I'm actually kind of bummed we won't be together at school, but I still think fifth grade is going to be AWESOME!

There are a lot of things my friends and I are excited about.

For the first time, we'll have homerooms (hopefully the same one!) and we'll get to switch classes. Plus, I got a cell phone! Chloe Jennifer already had one and so did some of my other friends, but mary Ann and Joey got them this summer too, which means now we'll all be able to text each other.

Even though school doesn't start for two more days, my phone is charged, my backpack is filled, and I've got new back-to-school shoes in my closet.

If you ask me, that's everything I need to make fifth grade the best year ever!

READY OR NOT?

It's Saturday morning and since school starts Monday, I have to decide what color to paint my nails.

It's a big decision, because I know Mary Ann will want to paint hers the same color. I open the drawer in my bathroom where I keep my nail-polish collection and try to decide on a color.

Light blue? Purple? Dark green?

I'm not sure.

I take my cell phone out of my pocket and send a text to my best friend. Mary Ann doesn't text right back, which probably means she's having as much trouble deciding as I am. Or maybe she's waiting for me to get to her house so we can decide together.

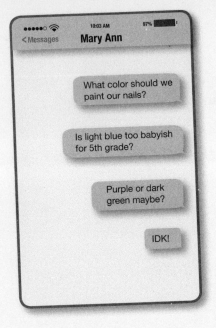

What color should we paint our nails?

Is light blue too babyish for 5th grade?

Purple or dark green maybe?

IDK!

We get together every year before school starts to make sure we're ready, and that's what we're doing today.

I grab a few of bottles of polish and stuff them into a bag. Then, I put Cheeseburger back on my bed and give her a goodbye pat. I walk to the kitchen to tell Mom I'm ready to go.

"Someone is excited!" says Mom when I walk into the kitchen.

"Mary Ann and I have a lot to do to get ready," I tell her.

Mom looks at Max, who is sitting at the table. He's busy texting, which is something he's been doing a lot of lately. "I'll be back in twenty minutes," Mom says to Max. But he doesn't look up.

"Are you texting Sam again?" I ask him. He texted her a lot on our trip to the Grand Canyon. I try to look over Max's shoulder, but he pulls his phone to his chest. That just confirms my suspicions.

I give my brother a *do-you-really-think-it's-a-good-idea-to-be-texting-a-girl-who-isn't-your-girlfriend* look. But Max ignores me and keeps texting.

I follow Mom outside. "I can't wait to get my schedule tomorrow. It's going to be so much fun to have homerooms. I really hope my friends and I are all in the same one," I tell her as we drive off.

Mom laughs. "I'm not sure you'll all be together, but I'm happy to see how enthusiastic you are," she says.

I'm not sure why, but I'm extra

enthusiastic about fifth grade. I just have a feeling it's going to be great. But when I get to Mary Ann's house, that feeling disappears as fast as butter melting on hot pancakes. I'm not the only person Mary Ann invited over.

"Hi," says Mary Ann. "Zoe's here too."

"Great!" I say. Part of me gets why Mary Ann invited Zoe. She lives a block away from the Winstons' new house, and we've always been friends with her. But the only people who've ever been part of our *getting-ready-to-go-back-to-school* sessions have been the two of us.

Plus, this is only the second time I've even seen Mary Ann since I got back from the Grand Canyon, and the first time was just for a few minutes when she stopped by my house so I could give her the mini-cactus I brought back for her.

Still, I don't want to make it seem like I'm unhappy that Zoe is here. When we get to Mary Ann's room, I pull the polishes I brought out of the bag.

"So, what color do you think we should paint our nails?" I ask Mary Ann.

Mary Ann gives me a funny look. "We're going to be in fifth grade. Our nails don't have to match." She shrugs. "It's kind of babyish."

I'm not sure if I should say we've always painted our nails the same color or if I should agree that having matching nails is kind of babyish. But before I say anything, I notice something on Mary Ann's wrist that hadn't been there the last time I saw her.

"Did you get a new bracelet?" I ask.

Mary Ann smiles. "Zoe gave it to me. It's from California. Isn't it cool?" She holds out her wrist for me to get a better look.

"My dad lives there," explains Zoe. "I spent the summer with him and he took me to a market where you can design your own jewelry."

When she talks she holds up her wrist and she's wearing the same kind of beaded bracelet that Mary Ann has on.

"Cool," I say. But Mary Ann wasn't nearly as excited about the gift I brought back for her from the Grand Canyon.

Which would YOU rather have??

I don't mind that she likes Zoe's present. What I don't get is why she doesn't want our nails to match, but doesn't mind that she and Zoe are wearing the same kind of bracelet.

Mary Ann and Zoe start talking about fifth grade teachers and who they want for homeroom. "I can't wait until tomorrow when we get the emails with our schedules!" says Zoe.

"I know! You have to call me as soon as you get yours," Mary Ann says.

I'm not sure if she's talking to Zoe, or to Zoe and me, but as they start to discuss what time they think we will get the emails, I feel like I'm not part of the conversation.

"I'm going to say hi to Joey," I tell them.

When I walk into his room, he's sitting on the floor organizing school supplies. "Hey!" he says. "Want to help?"

"Sure," I say and sit down next to him.

"So what's up with Zoe?" I ask as I take the wrapper off a package of pencils.

"She and Mary Ann hung out a lot while you were away. She's pretty cool," Joey says. "Everyone likes her, even Winnie."

"No way!" I say with a smile. Joey laughs. We both know Winnie never likes any of his or Mary Ann's friends.

As Joey and I start putting notebook paper in binders, Mary Ann sticks her head into Joey's room. "We're going to make smoothies. Do you guys want one?"

"I thought we were baking cookies," I say. Mary Ann and I ALWAYS bake cookies before school starts so we can take them in our lunches. We've NEVER made smoothies.

Mary Ann looks at Zoe who is standing beside her. "Zoe is into healthy eating. That's what she did all summer in California. I'm trying to eat healthy too."

Zoe smiles at Mary Ann like she's proud of her new habits.

"I'd rather drink a smoothie than organize school supplies," says Joey.

I don't want to be the only one who doesn't want one. Plus, smoothies taste good, and they're definitely healthier than cookies. "I'll have one too," I say.

As we start to walk to the kitchen, Zoe stops and knocks on Winnie's door. "Want a smoothie?" she asks.

"Sure," says Winnie. She comes out of her room and follows us to the kitchen.

I can't believe what I'm seeing! Winnie never wants to do anything with Mary Ann and me. The last time we asked her if she wanted to watch a movie, she said she'd rather spend a year alone on a desert island. Maybe Joey was right when he said Winnie likes Zoe. Or maybe she just likes smoothies. I don't know.

I watch quietly as Mary Ann fills the blender with strawberries, bananas, and ice. Zoe adds apple juice then blends everything together.

After Mary Ann pours the mixture into cups and passes them out, we sit at the table drinking our smoothies. When Winnie starts talking to Mary Ann and Zoe about back-to-school clothes and what she thinks would look cute on them, I'm even more surprised. It's one thing to want a smoothie, but it's a whole other thing for her to be acting so friendly toward us.

Finally, Joey says he has to finish organizing his school supplies and Winnie goes back to her room.

"Why don't we catch up on *Fashion Fran*?" I say to Mary Ann. She promised she'd record the episodes that aired while I was gone and that we'd watch them together.

Mary Ann puts the empty smoothie cups into the sink before she answers. "I'm kind of over *Fashion Fran*," she says.

"I've never liked that show," says Zoe.

But I ignore what Zoe said. I can't believe what just came out of my best friend's mouth. I'm not even sure it is her mouth.

I can't believe Mary Ann would ever say she's over our favorite

TV show. Zoe and Mary Ann and I go back to Mary Ann's room to hang out and look

at stuff on her computer. But I can't focus on music videos or online games.

All I can think about is that before I left on my trip, Mary Ann was my best friend. We liked doing all of the same things. Now, Mary Ann is doing new things like wearing beaded bracelets from California and drinking smoothies, and she's doing those things with Zoe.

Thinking about it makes me feel sick to my stomach, like I drank spoiled milk and not a fruit smoothie. That feeling stays with me when Dad comes to pick me up.

"Are you girls ready for school to start?" Dad asks when I get into the van.

I nod. Mary Ann might be ready. I went to her house to get prepared.

But I feel less ready than ever.

A BREAKUP

"Mallory, I have your schedule!" yells Mom.

I run from the family room to the kitchen. I've been waiting all morning for the email with my schedule to arrive. I stand behind Mom as she reads off my classes.

"Ms. Thompson for homeroom and language arts. Mr. Moreno, social studies. Mr. Hudson for math. And Mrs. Dunbar, science."

I know almost all of the teachers at
Fern Falls Elementary, but I've never heard
of my homeroom teacher. "Who is Ms.
Thompson?" I ask. Since Mom is the music
teacher at my school, she should know.

"Ms. Thompson is new," Mom says. "I met
her and I think you'll like her."

I let out a deep breath. "That's a relief!"
I say. Mom laughs as I race back to my

room. I plop down on my bed and start punching buttons on my phone.

I put my phone down on my bed beside Cheeseburger, and try not to look at it while I wait. Sometimes I think that makes people text back faster.

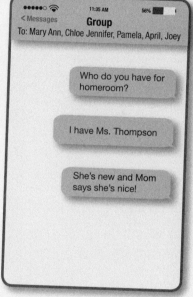

It works! Pamela and April text right back. They both have Mr. Hudson for homeroom. Joey texts back too. He's in Mrs. Dunbar's class and Chloe Jennifer texts that she's in Mr. Moreno's homeroom.

The only person who doesn't text back is Mary Ann.

It's kind of weird too because when I was at her house yesterday, she couldn't stop talking about how excited she was to find out who she has for homeroom.

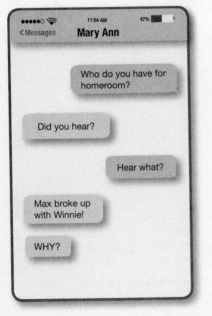

I take a deep breath and count to ten. I say the alphabet forwards and backwards. Still no text from Mary Ann. I can't imagine why it's taking her so long to answer.

I send Mary Ann another text.

I suck in my breath. I thought Mary Ann was going to text back about her homeroom teacher. I didn't think she was going to write that my brother broke up with her stepsister.

I'm not sure what to write back to Mary

Ann. I don't know what happened. I put my phone down and walk into Max's room. He's at his desk. I sit down on his bed and pat our dog, Champ, on the head. "What's going on?" I ask Max.

He looks at me like it's pretty obvious what's going on. "I'm putting school supplies into my backpack."

"Mary Ann told me you broke up with Winnie," I say.

Max shakes his head like he doesn't get why we're discussing this. "So?"

I clear my throat. "So I'm your sister, shouldn't I know when something big, like a breakup, happens in your life?"

Max rolls his eyes like that's the most ridiculous thing he's ever heard. "It's none of your business or Bird Brain's either."

Even though I don't like when my brother calls Mary Ann Bird Brain, I ignore it.

I have more important things on my mind. "When did you break up with her?" I ask.

"Which part of *it's none of your business* didn't you understand?"

"Max." I say his name in a soft way, not in a mad way. "I'm not trying to be nosy. But we talked about your girlfriend situation over the summer . . ."

Max laughs. "I didn't know it was a situation."

I shrug. "You know what I mean." I pause. "I guess I thought you might like telling someone what's going on."

Max nods, then lets out a breath. He actually looks like he's kind of glad to talk about it. "I just called her and did it," he says. "But I didn't say we were breaking up. I just said we were *taking a break*."

I'm not sure I see the difference. I think about Mary Ann's question. I start to ask

Max why he broke up with Winnie, but I think I know. "Does this have anything to do with Sam?"

Max sits up straight in his chair. "No comment," he says. Then he goes back to stuffing notebooks in his backpack. I can tell he's done talking.

I walk back to my room and pick up my phone. I'm still not sure what to text back to Mary Ann. But before I text anything, my phone rings.

My Conversation with Mary Ann

ME: (in a friendly voice) Hey!

MARY ANN: (in a not-so-friendly voice) So what happened?

ME: (hesitating, because even though I went in Max's room to find out what was going on, the way Mary Ann asked made me not want to tell her anything Max said.)

MARY ANN: (not waiting for me to say anything) Winnie said Max broke up with her and that it's just as well because she was going to break up with him anyway.

ME: (feeling relieved) It's good they broke up if they both wanted to.

MARY ANN: (sounding annoyed) I wouldn't call it good.

ME: (confused) Why not?

MARY ANN: (exhaling like she shouldn't have to explain it to me) He broke up with her the day before school starts. That's bad timing!

ME: (saying what was on my mind) I guess the timing could have been better. But if Winnie was going to break up with Max anyway, it doesn't seem like such a big deal.

MARY ANN: It's a big deal.

ME: (confused again) Why?

MARY ANN: (ignoring my question) So do

you know why he broke up with her?

ME: Max was busy. I don't think he was in the mood to talk. (changing the subject) So who did you get for homeroom? I have Ms. Thompson.

MARY ANN: I have Ms. Thompson too, and so does Zoe.

ME: Great!

Then Mary Ann said she had to go, and I said bye. But when we hung up, my stomach felt flip-floppy like it did yesterday when I was at her house.

It seemed like the only reason Mary Ann called me was to find out why Max broke up with Winnie. When I told her who I have for homeroom, she didn't even say she's glad we're in the same homeroom. All she said was that Zoe is in it too.

Even though I want to be in the same homeroom with all my friends, especially

Mary Ann, I kind of wish Zoe was in a different one. It's not that I don't like Zoe, but I'm starting to wonder if Zoe is becoming Mary Ann's new best friend.

I think about how Max told Winnie that they're *taking a break.* I guess that can happen between boyfriends and girlfriends. Can it happen between best friends too? I really hope not.

I don't want to start fifth grade without my best friend.

FIRST-DAY DRAMA

When I walk into the kitchen, I'm surprised to see what's on my plate.

"Blueberry pancakes?" I ask. Mom always makes chocolate chip pancakes on the first day of school.

Mom smiles. "I thought we'd start the year off with something different."

I like chocolate chip more than blueberry pancakes, but I want to start the year off with the right attitude.

"Thanks, Mom," I say with a smile. I eat my breakfast and then I pose with Max for our annual back-to-school photo.

But as I walk out the door, I.can't help but think that blueberries in my pancakes aren't the only thing that's different this year.

"Mallory!" Chloe Jennifer waves to me from her yard. I walk over to meet her so

we can walk to school together. It feels weird to not be walking to school with Mary Ann and Joey.

Even though a big part of me wishes they still lived on Wish Pond Road and were walking to school with us, it's hard not to feel excited as Chloe Jennifer loops her arm through mine. "We made the right choice," she says.

I know she's talking about what we're both wearing. I look down at our skirts. Chloe Jennifer texted Mary Ann and me last night. We texted back and forth for a long time until we all agreed to wear skirts for the first day of fifth grade. "We made the right choice," I say.

Chloe Jennifer giggles as we talk about how hard it was to decide.

"You're so lucky you're in Ms. Thompson's homeroom with Mary Ann,"

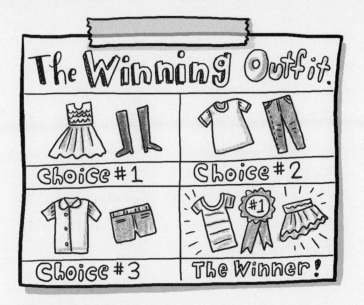

says Chloe Jennifer as we walk through the gates of Fern Falls Elementary.

I squeeze Chloe Jennifer's arm. I feel bad for her, since she doesn't have any close friends in her homeroom. "Mr. Moreno is really nice," I say. "He was Max's favorite teacher in fifth grade. And we'll all be together at lunch!" But as we part ways to walk to our homerooms, I think about

who's in mine. Even though I'm not sure
how glad I am that Zoe is with us, I'm
happy Mary Ann and I will be together.

That happiness drains right out of
me when I walk into Ms. Thompson's
classroom. Mary Ann is already there and
she isn't wearing a skirt like we all decided
we'd wear. She has on jeans and a T-shirt
with a scarf, and so does Zoe.

I walk over to where Mary Ann and Zoe are standing. "I thought you were wearing a skirt," I say to Mary Ann.

"I changed my mind," she says. "No big deal." But as Mary Ann and Zoe exchange a look, I feel like it is a big deal. I can tell they planned what to wear, and Mary Ann didn't tell Chloe Jennifer or me.

I'm glad when the bell rings and Ms. Thompson asks everyone to take a seat. "You may sit where you like," she says. "But if there is any trouble, I will rearrange the seating."

I pick a desk in the front row. Mary Ann sits down behind me. I watch as Zoe sits in the desk next to her.

"Welcome to fifth grade," says Ms. Thompson once everyone is sitting down.

I listen as she introduces herself. Ms. Thompson tells us she just moved to

Fern Falls from Oregon. She loves books, animals, baking, and hiking. She tells us that she's always loved reading and writing and that she's writing a book. "I'd like to start the year by giving you two writing assignments."

When she says that, some of the boys in the back of the class groan. But Ms. Thompson laughs. "Don't worry. They're easy assignments."

"I'd like each of you to write a one-page letter tonight telling me what you hope to accomplish in fifth grade." She explains that the letters will not only help us set goals but will also help her get to know us better.

"I'd also like each of you to bring in a notecard tomorrow morning with a question on it that you'd like to ask me. That way you will get to know me better too."

Since homeroom is short, we spend the rest of the time going around the room and introducing ourselves. I know everyone in my homeroom except for one boy who is new. His name is Devon and he just moved to Fern Falls. He has lots of red, curly hair and wants to be an actor or an architect or both when he grows up.

When the bell rings, we have a five-minute break before our next class, which is language arts with Ms. Thompson.

When language arts is over, I hop out of my seat and catch up to Mary Ann as she's walking out of the room. I want to get to her before Zoe does. "Isn't Ms. Thompson nice?" I say to Mary Ann.

"Very!" says Mary Ann.

"I'm really glad we have her," I say.

"Ms. Thompson is super cool!" says Zoe who walks up behind us.

Mary Ann smiles at Zoe. "Not as cool as the fact that we have math and then science together after language arts," she says like she forgot I'm standing here too.

First, Mary Ann and Zoe show up wearing jeans and scarves, even though Mary Ann, Chloe Jennifer, and I all agreed to wear skirts. Now, she's talking to Zoe like I'm not even part of the conversation. I can't help but wonder why.

I look down at my own schedule, which I glued to the back of one of my notebooks. I have social studies next and then P.E. It doesn't seem fair that Mary Ann and Zoe have all of their morning classes together.

Mary Ann and Zoe laugh as they walk down the hall together. I turn and walk the other way to my class.

I don't want to be dramatic on the first day of school, but I don't think fifth grade is off to such a good start.

TEACHER TROUBLE

I have good news and bad news.

The good news is that I worked hard on my essay last night, and I think it's really good. The other good news is that Mary Ann texted Zoe and me this morning. She wanted to know if we had our essays and questions ready. Zoe said she was all set. Now for the bad news: school starts in exactly twenty-eight minutes, and I still

don't know what I'm going to ask Ms.
Thompson in homeroom.

Mary Ann and Zoe both texted that
they'd help me figure something out
before class. I hope they'll give me
some inspiration.

I grab my backpack, my blank notecard,
and a banana before I head out the
door to meet Chloe Jennifer for our walk
to school.

When I get there, Mary Ann and Zoe are
already outside Ms. Thompson's classroom.
They're talking to Jackson, Pete, Danielle,
and Hannah. And they're all talking about
one thing—what they're going to ask
Ms. Thompson.

"I'm going to ask what her favorite food
is," says Pete.

"I'm asking about her favorite color,"
says Hannah.

"I'm going to ask what after-school activities she did when she was growing up," says Danielle.

"She said she's writing a book," says Jackson. "I'm going to ask her what her book is about."

"We have a two-part question," Zoe says. She looks at Mary Ann who smiles and nods. I try not to show that upsets me.

I'm not sure if it bothers me that they have a two-part question or if I'm just upset I don't have a question at all.

Jackson looks at me. "Mallory, what are you going to ask?"

"I don't know," I say.

"You should ask something personal," says Zoe. "Ms. Thompson said she wants us to ask questions so we get to know her better."

"Like what?" I ask. But the bell rings

so there's no time for anyone to answer my question.

"Good morning, everyone," Ms. Thompson says once we're all seated. She takes attendance then says it's time for our questions. "Who would like to go first?" she asks.

Devon raises his hand. "If you were an animal, what would you be?"

"Great question!" says Ms. Thompson.

I try not to groan. That was only the first question and it was a good one.

"If I could be any animal, I would definitely be a bird. I'd love to be able to fly," says Ms. Thompson.

As she goes around the room, I listen while my classmates ask all kinds of questions, like what her favorite TV show is and if she has a pet and what she likes to bake. A lot of these questions are questions

I thought about asking. But I don't want to ask what's already been asked.

Think, Mallory.

When Ms. Thompson gets to Mary Ann, she announces that she and Zoe have a two-part question. Ms. Thompson smiles and says they are the first students who have ever asked a two-part question.

"Why did you want to be a teacher?" Mary Ann asks Ms. Thompson.

She explains that she likes helping kids learn and that she especially likes helping kids discover books that are meaningful to them. Then she calls on Zoe who asks the second part of their question.

"Do you like teaching fifth grade?" Zoe asks.

Ms. Thompson smiles. I try to listen as she talks about how much she likes teaching fifth grade. But I can't focus on

what she's saying. I need to think of a
question and FAST. It's my turn!

"Mallory," says Ms. Thompson.

I think about Zoe's advice. *Ask
something personal.*

I ask the first thing that comes to mind.
"Are you married?" I blurt out.

Ms. Thompson's smile disappears.
"Mallory, that's a rather personal
question," she says. "But the answer is no. I
am not married."

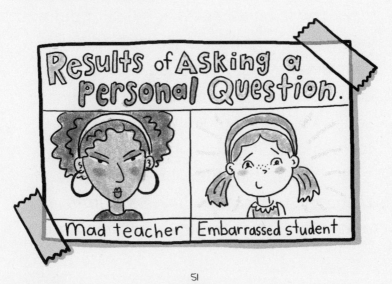

I hear a few giggles from the back of the class.

I can feel my face turning red. I asked my new teacher something she didn't like hearing. It's only the second day of class, and I'm already off on the wrong foot.

After homeroom I walk up to Zoe and Mary Ann. "I wish you hadn't told me to ask something personal," I say to Zoe.

"I'm sorry," says Zoe. "I didn't mean to ask her something *too* personal."

I know it's not her fault. But that doesn't mean I'm not still embarrassed. At lunch, I tell Pamela what happened. "Don't worry," says Pamela between bites of her tuna sandwich. "I'm sure Ms. Thompson will forget about it by tomorrow."

But I'm not so sure. She looked pretty unhappy. I try to eat the peanut butter and marshmallow sandwich Mom packed for me. But it sticks in my throat.

It's only day two of the new year and I'm already having teacher trouble.

As I walk to math, which is my first class after lunch, I think about the letter I wrote last night. Ms. Thompson wanted to know what our goals are for fifth grade. What I wanted to write was that my goal was to keep my best friend.

But I didn't think that was the kind of goal Ms. Thompson had in mind. So I wrote that I want fifth grade to be the best year ever and that my goal is to make all A's. But I think I need to revise my letter. My new goal is pretty simple.

I just want to stay on my teacher's good side.

WEEKEND WOES

If I had to rate the first week of school a thumbs-up or a thumbs-down, I'd give it a thumbs sideways.

Some good things happened. I like all of my classes—especially Mr. Moreno's social studies class. The theme of our year in social studies is *The World Around Us*. Our first unit is about states and capitals, which sounds like it could be boring, but not with Mr. Moreno.

He plays the guitar and he has a song for every state. He already sang us his "A" state song, which was about Alabama, Alaska, Arizona, and Arkansas.

I wasn't the only one who liked his song. When he finished singing, everyone in my class clapped and cheered like we were at a concert.

ROCK STAR TEACHER.

In art, Mrs. Pearl said we are making life-size papier-mâché sculptures of dogs and cats. I brought in a picture of Cheeseburger and asked her if I could make my sculpture of my cat and she said yes. I can't wait to have a sculpture of Cheeseburger in my room!

And best of all, Ms. Thompson seemed to have forgotten the question I asked her. She didn't bring it up again. And it didn't seem like she was upset with me either.

Unfortunately, some not-so-good things happened this week too.

Mary Ann and Zoe were practically inseparable. Whenever I saw them at school, they were together.

I tried to be friendly. And it wasn't like they weren't friendly back. At least Zoe was. But every time I was around them, Mary Ann acted like I wasn't even there. And Thursday night when I texted Mary Ann and Chloe Jennifer to see if they wanted to sleep over, Mary Ann never responded.

I thought maybe the problem was that Mary Ann didn't see my text.

When I got to school on Friday, I asked if she wanted to sleep over, but she told me she had other plans.

After homeroom, I watched her talking to Zoe and I knew what those plans were. Thinking about the fun things they would be doing without me made me feel like I had just watched a sad movie.

That feeling stayed with me all afternoon, and even last night. When Chloe Jennifer came over, she asked if everything was OK.

"I'm fine," I told her.

"Are you upset that Mary Ann isn't sleeping over?" she asked.

I wasn't sure what to say. I didn't want Chloe Jennifer to think I wasn't happy that she was sleeping over. "A little bit, I guess."

Chloe Jennifer nodded like she got it. "Me too. It's kind of weird how Mary Ann has been spending all her time with Zoe."

As Chloe Jennifer and I talked about how close Mary Ann and Zoe seem to be getting, I felt bad that I hadn't thought about how this was making Chloe Jennifer feel.

Chloe Jennifer and Mary Ann aren't best friends, like Mary Ann and I are. But they are close. When Chloe Jennifer first moved to Wish Pond Road, we both hung out with her a lot. Now Mary Ann is spending even less time with her than she's spending with me.

"We can have fun without Mary Ann,"
I said.

"Of course we can," said Chloe Jennifer.

And we did. We popped popcorn and watched a movie and stayed up late talking about all the fun things that are happening this year at school that we have to look forward to, like Pajama Day in two weeks.

But when Chloe Jennifer left, it was hard not to think about how Mary Ann didn't want to come to the sleepover.

I think Mom could tell something was wrong because she asked if I wanted to go to the mall. She knew I needed a cover for my phone and offered to buy me one.

"Can I come too?" asked Max.

I was surprised Max wanted to come, but we all piled into the van for a family outing to the Fern Falls Mall.

On the way there, I was starting to feel

better. It was sweet of Mom to offer to take me and I was excited to get a phone cover. "Can we go to the kiosk that sells phone covers first?" I asked Mom.

"Sure," she said. I expected Max to say he wanted to go to the sporting goods store first, but he didn't argue.

When we got there, everything was fine. Mom and I started looking at the selection of phone cases. There were so many cute

ones. I made a pile of the ones I liked best—a purple-and-pink-striped one, a leopard-print case and a blue one with rhinestones.

I couldn't decide which one I wanted. Even though Max

is no cute-phone-case expert, I turned around to ask his opinion. But when I did, Max was busy talking to a girl. She was wearing a baseball cap, but I could tell she had a face full of freckles.

"Mallory, this is Sam," said Max.

I was starting to get why Max said he wanted to come to the mall. "*The* Sam?" I asked. As soon as the words left my mouth, I wanted to stuff them back in.

I thought Max was going to get upset, but Sam laughed like she thought it was funny and that made Max laugh too.

"Wow! I'm famous!" said Sam.

I let out a breath and smiled. I was glad Max wasn't mad about what I'd said. "So which phone case do you like?" I pointed to the pile I'd made on the counter.

Max shook his head like he didn't have an opinion. But Sam did. "I like the striped one," she said.

I was just about to say, "Me too." But before I could, I saw Mary Ann, Zoe, and Winnie walking towards the phone-cover kiosk. I'm not sure they had planned to stop, but it would have been weird if they hadn't.

"Hi," I said like I was glad to see them. Zoe was the only one who said hi back.

Mary Ann looked at me like she couldn't imagine what I was doing at the mall—even though going to the mall is something she knows I love doing.

I looked at Mary Ann like my feelings were hurt that she hadn't come to my sleepover last night, and hadn't invited me to come to the mall with her.

Winnie looked at Max like he was the last person on the planet she wanted to see. Then she looked at Sam like she was the second-to-last person she wanted to see.

Max looked like he'd rather be anywhere than at the mall with Sam *and* Winnie.

Sam smiled at Winnie. "So what are you guys up to?" she asked.

"Huh?" said Winnie like that was a ridiculous question to ask, even though it wasn't. It was pretty clear that Sam was just trying to be friendly.

It was also clear that Winnie had no intention of being friendly back, even though she and Sam are in the same grade at school and seem to know each other.

Max opened his mouth like he wanted to say something, but had no idea what to say.

Everybody was just standing there looking at everybody else in this weird way. Finally, Mom broke the silence. "Do you know which phone cover you want?" she asked.

"Yeah," I said. I grabbed one off the counter and handed it to Mom.

"You sure you want this one?" she asked. "It's kind of plain."

I looked down at the gray case in Mom's hand. I didn't even care what it looked like. I just wanted to get out of the mall.

I saw Winnie poke Mary Ann as Mom was paying. "We have to go," she said like they had somewhere important to be. Mom finished paying and I watched them walk off together, whispering and laughing.

"That was weird," Sam said once they'd walked away.

"Yeah, sorry about that," said Max.

Sam shrugged. "No big deal," she said. Then she told us she had to meet her mom, who was waiting for her.

We all said bye, but as I walked to the van with Mom and Max, I couldn't help thinking that what had happened was a big deal, at least to me. As I thought about it, my eyes filled with tears and my head filled with questions.

The Questions in My Head,
by Mallory McDonald

Question #1: Why were Mary Ann, Zoe, and Winnie acting so weird at the mall?

Question #2: Why didn't Mary Ann ask me if I wanted to go to the mall with them?

Question #3: As Mary Ann, Zoe, and Winnie walked off, were they talking about me or the fact that Max was talking to Sam?

Question #4: Why was Max talking to Sam?
Does Max like Sam? Does Sam like Max?
(Three questions but they all kind of belong together.)

Question #5: Is Winnie going to be
mad if Max likes another girl?

Question #6: Is Mary Ann going to be mad
for Winnie if Max likes another girl?

Question #7: If Max likes another girl,
is Mary Ann going to decide she doesn't
want to be my best friend anymore?

Question #8: Has Mary Ann already decided that?

Question #9: If she has decided that, does
it even have anything to do with Max?

Question #10: Or does it have
everything to do with Zoe?

As I got into the van, those questions kept going around and around in my brain. I just couldn't figure out why Mary Ann was acting like we're hardly friends. I tried to think if I'd done something to make her mad, but I couldn't think of one thing.

When Mom got into the van, she handed me the bag with my new phone cover in it. I took it out of the package. Then I added one more question to my list.

Why did I buy such an ugly phone cover?

FROM BAD
TO WORSE

Monday isn't my favorite day of the week, but I'm happy it's here. Hopefully this week will be a lot better than the weekend.

On Saturday, after I saw Mary Ann at the mall with Zoe and Winnie, I waited for her to call me. I thought for sure she'd say something like: *Mallory, I know it was kind of weird running into each other. I'm sorry if I've been a bad best friend lately.*

But Mary Ann didn't call on Saturday. Or Sunday. We always talk on the weekends so I thought about calling her. The truth is that there were some things I wanted to say to her like: *Why have you been a bad best friend lately? Is Zoe your new best friend? Does that mean we're not friends anymore?*

But I didn't call her. Even though I had questions, I wasn't sure I was ready to hear the answers.

Plus, I didn't want to make it seem like I thought it was a big deal that she didn't call me all weekend. And maybe it wasn't?

YOUR BEST FRIEND doesn't call all weekend. CHECK ONE:
___ Big Deal
___ No Big Deal

As I walk into Ms. Thompson's classroom,
I decide not to make it into one.

Mary Ann is already in the room talking
to Zoe and Danielle. I walk over to where
they're standing. "Hey," I say in a friendly
voice like nothing is wrong.

"Hi," says Mary Ann. She smiles.

"Are you ready for the vocab test?" I
ask everyone.

"I am," says Danielle.

"Me too," says Mary Ann.

Zoe nods like she is too, and then
changes the subject. "How do you like your
new phone cover?" she asks.

"You got a new phone cover?" asks
Danielle. "Can I see it?"

"Sure," I say. I don't really like the
cover I got, but I take my phone out of my
backpack and show it to Danielle.

"I like it," says Danielle.

"Me too," says Zoe. "Simple, but cool."

"Yeah," says Mary Ann like she agrees.

"Thanks," I say smiling. But my smile fades fast.

"Mallory, may I see you at my desk please?" says Ms. Thompson.

I know why Ms. Thompson wants to see me. I quickly try to shove my phone in my backpack, but it's too late. "Mallory, you know you're not allowed to have your phone out during class," says Ms. Thompson when I get to her desk.

"I'm sorry," I say. I feel my face turning red. I must look like a giant tomato.

I try to explain to Ms. Thompson that I only got it out to show my friends my new cover, but Ms. Thompson isn't interested in my explanation.

"I'm disappointed that you would break the rules." She looks at me like she's waiting for her words to sink in. Then she reaches out her hand. "Phone, please."

I give Ms. Thompson my phone. When she takes the roll, all I can think about is if she's going to tell Mom, and if Mom is going to be mad. Since she's a teacher at Fern Falls Elementary, I know she expects me to follow all of the rules. But I didn't mean to break this one! And who knows when I'm going to get my phone back?

I'm still thinking about it in language arts.

When Ms. Thompson calls out the words on the vocab test, I can't even remember how to spell *horrific,* which was a word I could spell perfectly last night. But I do remember the meaning of it and I can use it in a sentence.

Having my phone taken by my teacher is horrific!!!

When we finish taking our test, Ms. Thompson tells us about our first book report of the year.

"This is going to be a partner project. I'd like each of you to choose a partner and then a book. You and your partner will read the book, and then you'll choose a scene from the book to act out in front of the class. We're going to have a contest. Everyone in the class will vote for the best presentation."

Ms. Thompson pauses and smiles. "There will be prizes for the winning team."

Then she tells everyone to start picking partners.

I turn to Mary Ann who is sitting in the row behind me. "Want to be partners?"

She looks at Zoe who is sitting beside her. "Sorry," she says. "Zoe and I are already partners."

I don't see how they could have already decided to be partners because I asked Mary Ann if she wanted to be partners as soon as Ms. Thompson said it was time to pick.

"If you don't have a partner, please raise your hand," says Ms. Thompson.

I realize I'm in that group. I raise my hand and look around the room. The only other person with his hand up is the new boy, Devon.

"Mallory and Devon, you two can be partners," says Ms. Thompson. Then she passes around a list of suggested books and says that we can have a few minutes with our partners to select a book.

Devon pulls a chair up next to my desk and puts the list on it. "What do you think we should pick?" he asks.

"Let's look," I say. I try to focus on the list of books, but that's not so easy to do. I hear Mary Ann and Zoe talking behind me about the book they're going to pick.

I can't believe Mary Ann picked Zoe to be her partner.

"How about *Holes*?" I hear Devon say.

"Sure," I tell him. I've heard it's a good book.

But my brain isn't thinking about the book. It's thinking about this week. It's only Monday morning and my teacher has already taken my phone, I missed a word on my vocab test, and my best friend picked someone else to be her partner for the book report project.

I think about the book Devon and I picked: *Holes.*

Right now, I'd like to find a great big one and climb into it.

OH BROTHER!

I walk into Max's room. "Can I talk to you?" I ask. I plop down on his bed without waiting for an answer.

Max is sitting at his desk, texting, and Champ is asleep beside him. I wait for my brother to look up, but he doesn't.

"Max." I say my brother's name again. "This is important! All week at school, Mary Ann and Zoe have been inseparable. And I'm not the only one who's noticed. Chloe

Jennifer and Pamela both said they think it's weird how all of a sudden, Mary Ann and Zoe are acting like best friends. I feel like I'm losing my best friend."

I finish talking, and wait for Max to speak. He usually doesn't have much to say when it comes to Mary Ann. Still, I'm hoping he'll have some big-brotherly advice on what I can do to get my best friend back. I could sure use some. But Max doesn't even look up. He has a big smile on his face.

I walk over to where he's sitting, pick up a folder off his desk and bop him on the head with it. "EARTH TO MAX!"

"Huh?" he says like he just realized I'm in his room.

I blow a piece of hair off my face. "What are you doing that's so important you can't listen to me?"

Finally Max looks at me like he's paying attention. "I just asked Sam if she wants to go out."

"On a date?"

Max rolls his eyes at me like that's a dumb question. "No, like go out. And she said yes. So we are." Then Max goes right back to texting and grinning.

What do I say? *Congratulations? Sam seems great?* But I can't worry about what to say to Max when I have my own problems.

I go back to my own room to try to figure out what to do. All week I've been ignoring the fact that Mary Ann hasn't been a good best friend to me. I've tried to act like it's no big deal. But it is a BIG deal.

And I don't think this new development is going to help.

Mary Ann was upset when Winnie and Max broke up. I have a feeling she's going to be even more upset when she hears Max has a new girlfriend. I sit down on my bed and look at Cheeseburger. I need to do something to remind Mary Ann that we're supposed to be friends, not enemies. I rub my head, but it doesn't help me think.

I pick up *Holes*. Maybe reading will help me forget about my problems for a while.

I only have three more chapters before the end. I read until I finish. It's easy to do because *Holes* is a very good book.

Then I put my book down. "I have a great idea," I say to Cheeseburger. I don't know why I didn't think of it before. I pick up my phone and start typing.

I put my phone down. All I need to do now is wait for Mary Ann to text me back. Even though I know she thinks it's babyish to match, I think she'll think wearing matching pajamas on Pajama Day is a different story.

For as long as we've been friends,

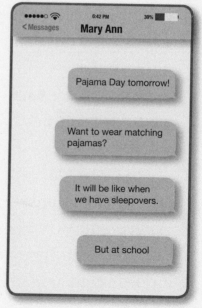

we've been wearing matching pajamas when we have sleepovers. We have lots of matching pajamas we could wear. The hardest part will be deciding which ones we want to wear.

Just thinking about it makes me feel better.

But when Mary Ann texts back, my good feelings fade fast. She doesn't say anything about pajamas.

Ugh! This is exactly what I was afraid would happen.

I get why Mary Ann would be upset. Winnie and Max went out for a long time. It does seem kind of fast for Max to start

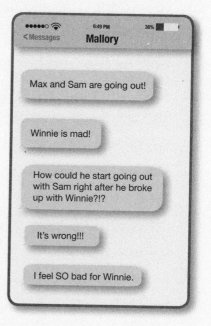

going out with somebody else. Plus, now that Winnie and Mary Ann have gotten close, I get why she would take Winnie's side.

Max is NOT helping my friendship with Mary Ann.

I march back into the bathroom where he's brushing his teeth and give him the facts. "Max, Winnie is mad at you because you're going out with Sam. That means Mary Ann is mad too. And the person Mary Ann is mad at, besides you, is me!"

Max looks at me like I'm an alien from outer space and nothing I just said makes any sense. "That's ridiculous," says Max.

"Mary Ann won't want to be friends with me anymore."

"You should be happy to be done with Bird Brain," says Max.

Max might not like my best friend, but I do. I don't want Mary Ann to be mad. "I thought you said you and Winnie were just taking a break."

Max rolls his eyes. "I don't want to talk about this," he says. He wipes his mouth with a towel and starts to walk back to his room like the conversation is over.

But I'm not done talking. "How would

you feel if your best friend was mad at you for something that wasn't even your fault?"

Max looks at me. "I would feel like that person wasn't being a very good friend."

I go back to my room, but I keep thinking about what Max said. Maybe he's right, but it doesn't make me feel better. I have a math test I haven't studied for. And I have to pick out the pajamas I'm going to be wearing tomorrow.

Even though I won't have anyone to match with.

PAJAMA PROBLEMS

I'm not keeping a diary, at least not right now. But if I did, here's what I'd write about my day.

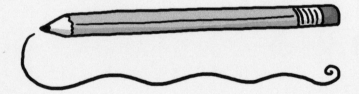

Dear Diary,

Today was Pajama Day at school. I didn't think it would be a big deal. You just show up wearing pajamas. Right?

Wrong!

That's what I did, and what most of the kids at Fern Falls Elementary did too. But it's not what Mary Ann and Zoe did. They showed up wearing *the same* pajamas.

They both had on blue tie-dyed pajamas.

Mary Ann and Zoe... who match!!!

When I asked Mary Ann if she wanted to wear matching pajamas, she never even responded. She's made it pretty clear lately that she wants Zoe to be her new best friend. I can't say I was surprised when I saw them wearing the same pajamas.

But what did surprise me were the pajamas they were wearing. I never even knew Mary Ann had those pajamas. She and Zoe must have bought them together, which meant they must have planned to match on Pajama Day.

The day I went to Mary Ann's house to get ready for school, she said matching was babyish. But it seems like she only meant matching with *me* is babyish.

During the break between homeroom and language arts, I went up to Mary Ann. "New pajamas?" I asked.

"Yeah," said Mary Ann.

"Did you and Zoe plan to match?" I asked.

"It was a total coincidence," said Mary Ann. Then the bell rang, so I had to sit down. But I felt worse than I had before. It was just really hard for me to believe that it was a coincidence.

Writing that makes it sound like I thought Mary Ann was lying. I don't like writing that I thought someone was lying to me (especially when the person I'm talking about is supposed to be my best friend). So I'll just say this—I wasn't convinced she was telling the truth.

And it bothered me. A LOT!

It was bad enough that she didn't want to wear matching pajamas with me. But it was even worse that she hadn't been honest with me about it.

In language arts, Ms. Thompson told us that we could use class time to work with our partners on our book reports.

"As you and your partner discuss your book, try to identify the problem that the main character in the book is having," said Ms. Thompson.

But as I sat down to work with Devon, I watched Mary Ann and Zoe sit down to work on their book report. I wasn't thinking about the problem Stanley Yelnats was having in *Holes*. I was thinking about the problem I was having at Fern Falls Elementary.

I've tried to ignore the problem with Mary Ann. I've tried to pretend like my feelings aren't hurt. But I can't just keep ignoring or pretending.

Devon waved his hands in front of my face like he was trying to get my

attention. "I know
you're thinking
about something
and it's not *Holes*,"
said Devon.

Hard to focus on this!

HOLES

"You're right," I
admitted. I hadn't
planned to tell him
what happened.
But he looked
like he could tell I
needed someone to talk to.

I lowered my voice to a whisper and
told him Mary Ann and I have always
been best friends but now it seems like
she wants to be best friends with Zoe.

I told him about some of the stuff she
has done lately, including the fact that I
asked if she wanted to wear matching
pajamas today and she never even

answered, and
then showed up
wearing the same
pajamas as Zoe.
I told him that
she said it was a
coincidence but
that I didn't think
it was.

Good Talker

And I told him how Max broke up
with Winnie and is going out with Sam,
and now Winnie is
mad at Max, which
makes Mary Ann
mad at me.

Good
Listener

Devon listened
patiently while I
told him everything.
"Wow!" he said
when I was done.

"That's more complicated than the plot of *Holes*."

That made me smile. It wasn't actually true, because a lot of crazy stuff happens in that book. But it was funny, and I could tell that he was trying to make me feel better. "It is kind of complicated," I said.

"And dumb," said Devon. "Mary Ann doesn't have a reason to be mad at you. Max can go out with whoever he wants to go out with."

Hearing Devon say that made me realize he was right.

Even though I had kind of agreed with Mary Ann when she texted me that it was wrong of Max to start going out with Sam right after he broke up with Winnie, Mary Ann shouldn't be mad at me for that.

"I get that," I said to Devon. "But Mary Ann doesn't seem to."

"Explain it to her," said Devon. "Tell her how you feel."

"You're right," I said. "I've been thinking about doing that. I just have to decide what to say."

"Just say what's on your mind." Then Devon said something that surprised me. "I'm the youngest of five boys. If I don't speak up when I have something to say, no one would know what I want. I'm not even sure anyone would know I'm alive."

I thought about what he'd just told me. I just have one older brother. It has its good moments, but it can be hard too. "Having four older brothers must be tough sometimes," I said.

Devon nodded. "It can be."

Then I looked at Devon. He has a head full of bright red, curly hair. "But it would be pretty hard not to know you're alive," I said.

I guess Devon knew exactly what I was talking about. He laughed and then said, "All of my brothers have the same hair as I do."

Devon

#1   #2   #3   #4   #5

I tried to picture Devon and his brothers. Picturing them was easy.

I hope talking to Mary Ann will be easy too.

"T" IS FOR TERRIBLE

"T" is for "talk" and for "terrible." Or in this case, a "terrible talk."

That's the kind of talk I just had with Mary Ann. All afternoon, I thought about what Devon said about how he has to speak up or no one will know what he wants.

What I want is for Mary Ann to be my best friend, just like she's always been, but I also want her to know that she's done a lot of things that have hurt my feelings. So when I got home from school, I called Mary Ann. She finally answered on the fifth ring.

And here's what happened.

My Talk with Mary Ann

ME: Hey.

MARY ANN: (sounding like I woke her up which I knew I hadn't because she'd just gotten home from school and no one takes a nap right when they get home from school) Hey.

ME: (in a friendly voice) What's up?

MARY ANN: (in an unfriendly voice) Not much.

ME: (annoyed Mary Ann wasn't being friendly, especially after she was the one who wore matching pajamas with someone

else, lied about it, and has done a lot of things lately that don't fall into the "friendly" category) It hurt my feelings that you and Zoe wore matching pajamas today.

MARY ANN: (acting like she couldn't believe I'd said that) It wasn't a big deal.

ME: I asked you if you wanted to wear matching pajamas and you never even answered me. Then, you and Zoe showed up wearing them.

MARY ANN: I told you the pajamas were just a coincidence.

ME: It didn't seem like a coincidence.

MARY ANN: Well, it was.

ME: (changing the subject because I

knew Mary Ann wasn't going to admit that it wasn't a coincidence) Are you mad at me because Max broke up with Winnie then started going out with Sam?

MARY ANN: (blowing out a breath) Kind of.

ME: Why are you mad at me for that?

MARY ANN: (finally answering) I just feel bad for Winnie.

ME: You said she was going to break up with Max anyway. Even if what Max did was wrong, that's not my fault.

MARY ANN: That's not the issue.

ME: What's the issue? Is it that you don't want to be best friends anymore?

MARY ANN: (talking like she was talking

to someone really young or really stupid)
We'll always be friends, but that doesn't
mean we can't be friends with other people.

ME: (trying not to talk like I was talking
to someone really young or really stupid) I
get that. We've always had other friends.
But all of a sudden, you don't want to
do any of the things we've always loved
doing like painting our nails the same color
or wearing matching clothes or baking
cookies or watching *Fashion Fran*—

MARY ANN: (cutting me off like I was
done, which I wasn't) I'm just not as
babyish as I used to be. We're in fifth
grade. I guess I don't like doing a lot of the
stuff I used to like doing. Is there anything
wrong with that?

ME: It's not just that. When I invited you
to a sleepover with Chloe Jennifer and me,
you didn't want to come. You didn't ask me

to go to the mall when you and Zoe and Winnie went. And when I asked you if you wanted to be partners for the book report project, you picked Zoe—

MARY ANN: (cutting me off again even though I still wasn't done) We don't have to do everything together.

ME: But you act like you don't want to do *anything* with me. Do you not want to be friends anymore?

MARY ANN: That's not it.

ME: Then what is it?

MARY ANN: I've already tried to explain it. I don't know what else to say. I have to go.

So all I said was bye, and then we hung up. But thinking about it makes me sad.

Mary Ann and I have been friends since we were babies. We grew up next door to each other. When we were little, we used to play chase in our backyards.

The beginning of a long friendship.

When we got older, we started doing other things like painting our nails and having sleepovers and watching *Fashion Fran*. No matter, what we did, we always liked doing it together. I never thought that wouldn't be the case.

When I moved to Fern Falls, Mary Ann threw a goodbye party for me and we were both so sad that we wouldn't live next door to each other anymore.

Then, her mom and Joey's dad met and fell in love and got married. Mary Ann and her mom moved to Fern Falls. We were so happy to be neighbors again. We've done so many fun things together.

But so much has changed. It's not just that Mary Ann moved to a new house across town. She's different than she used to be. It makes me sad that our friendship is changing, but it makes me even more sad that she doesn't seem to know—or doesn't care—that she has done things that hurt my feelings.

I put my phone on my nightstand and curl up on my bed with Cheeseburger.

It would be great if I could do something simple to make things go back to being the way they've always been. But I know there's no magic cure. I think about all the times I went to the wish pond and made wishes when I wanted something to happen. Lately, I haven't gone. The truth is I'm not sure the wish pond works anyway.

I don't know what will work. I reach over to my nightstand for a tissue, and Cheeseburger nuzzles into me. She can tell I'm upset.

I called Mary Ann so I would feel better, but I feel worse than ever.

BONDING TIME

"May I come in?"

I look up. Max is standing in my doorway. He doesn't wait for an answer. He walks into my room, pulls my desk chair up to my bed, and sits down.

I try to wipe my eyes without him noticing.

"I heard your conversation. It stinks that Mary Ann is mad at you because I broke up with Winnie then started going out with Sam," says Max.

I don't even bother to ask Max why he was eavesdropping. I think about what Devon said. "I don't mind if you go out with Sam," I say. "She seems really nice."

Max nods like he appreciates what I'm saying. "I don't know what Mary Ann said. I only heard your part of the conversation. But none of this is any of her business." Max keeps talking. "I bet Mary Ann didn't tell you Winnie already has a new boyfriend."

I shake my head. I didn't know that. Winnie must not be too upset if she already has a new boyfriend. Even though I get that it's dumb Mary Ann is mad at me for something that happened between Max and Winnie, it's only part of the problem.

I pick a fuzz ball off my blanket.

"What is it?" asks Max like he gets that there's something I'm not saying.

I tell Max about how it seems like Mary Ann wants Zoe to be her new best friend. "I don't think she wants to be friends with me anymore." I look down and pick at another fuzz ball. "I know you don't like her, but she's been my best friend my whole life. It's kind of hard to just stop wanting to be friends with her."

Max listens while I'm talking and doesn't interrupt. "I get it," he says when I'm done. "It sounds like she's going through a phase."

I wrinkle my nose. "Huh?" I ask. I'm not sure what Max means.

"Mary Ann is going through a phase. A Zoe phase. Everyone goes through phases," he says.

"Can you give me some examples?"

Max scratches his head like he's thinking. "There's this kid, Jake, on my baseball team. He's our best pitcher. Last week, he showed up at practice and told the coach he's sick of pitching and wants to play third base."

"How do you know it's a phase? Maybe Jake will never want to pitch again."

Max shakes his head from side to side like that's ridiculous. "Jake loves pitching. He'll pitch again."

I see Max's point. He thinks Mary Ann is just going through a phase where she wants to be best friends with Zoe, and then she'll get tired of that and want to be best friends with me again. But I'm not so sure. "How can you tell if someone is going through a phase?" I ask.

Max smiles. "People go through them all the time. Remember how Dad had a beard when we were little and now he doesn't?"

I nod. It was scratchy and I didn't like the way it felt when he hugged or kissed me. I was really glad when he shaved it off.

"I get it," I tell Max. I pause. "But it's more than that."

Two Phases of Dad.

Phase 1　Phase 2

Max raises a brow like he's waiting for me to explain, so I do.

"Mary Ann has done a lot of stuff lately that really hurt my feelings." I tell Max about the book report Mary Ann and Zoe are doing together, and how they wore matching pajamas on Pajama Day, and that she didn't want to sleep over when I invited her. "I want to be friends with her, but not if she's going to act like that."

"People can be unpredictable," says Max. "Sometimes they do things you don't like. Hopefully Mary Ann will see that she hasn't been acting like a very good friend."

I can feel the tears starting to form in my eyes again. "What if she doesn't?"

Max smiles. "Want some advice?"

I nod again.

"Keep being a good friend to Mary Ann, just like you've always been." Then he pauses. "She has other friends and so do you. You should focus on those friends too."

I sit for a minute and think about what my brother said. It makes sense. And it gives me an idea. A great idea!

"You're right. I'm going to focus on Mary Ann *and* my other friends. I know how I'm going to do it too." Then I flash a smile at him. "And you're part of my plan."

Max stops smiling. "Oh no! I'm not sure what you have in mind, but I'm pretty sure I'm not going to like it."

I explain to Max exactly what I have in mind. "Will you help me?" I ask when I'm done explaining.

"Count me in," says Max.

He starts walking toward the door like our talk is over.

"Hey Max," I say. He stops and turns around. "Thanks for being a good big brother."

"Anytime," says Max as he leaves my room.

I pick up Cheeseburger and put her in my lap.

Max has never been such a nice big brother. Maybe he felt bad when he heard me on the phone with Mary Ann. Maybe we're getting older and closer. Or maybe it has something to do with us going to different schools.

Who knows? Maybe he's just going through a phase.

I really hope not, though.

CAMP MALLORY

When Max and I had our talk, I came up with an idea. I decided to invite a bunch of my friends, including Zoe, to come to my house this weekend. I told them I had a big surprise in store for them. But that was all I told them.

Even Mary Ann. Things have been weird since we had our talk on Pajama Day. It seems like it's something we're just not going to talk about.

Still, I know she's excited about my surprise.

Ever since I told my friends I have a surprise for them, she's been asking me what's going on, but I told her she'd have to wait to find out, just like everyone else.

The big day is finally here. I'm excited, but a little nervous. I hope my friends will like what I planned. I pick up my phone and send a text.

When I hear the doorbell ring, I race from my room to answer it. Pamela arrives first, then April and Chloe

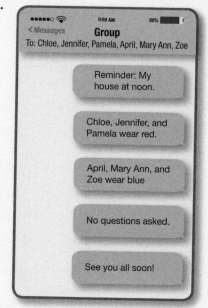

●●●●●○ 📶   9:59 AM   88% ▬▬ �

< Messages   **Group**

To: Chloe, Jennifer, Pamela, April, Mary Ann, Zoe

Reminder: My house at noon.

Chloe, Jennifer, and Pamela wear red.

April, Mary Ann, and Zoe wear blue

No questions asked.

See you all soon!

Jennifer. Mary Ann and Zoe are the last ones to show up.

"So what's the surprise?" asks Mary Ann.

"I'm glad you asked!" I say. I lead my friends outside to my backyard. "Welcome to Camp Mallory!" I say.

I watch as my friends look around at everything Max and I set up. There's a sign

and a tent and even an area with athletic
equipment and a score board Max made.

"Wow!" says Mary Ann. "It does look like
camp!" She smiles at me and I smile back.
I know that's her way of saying that even
though we've had our differences lately,
one thing we'll always agree on is that we
both love camp.

"Thanks," I say as I pass out bandanas and water bottles to everyone. "We're having a mini color war," I tell my friends. "It's red vs. blue."

When Max comes outside and explains that he's the referee, I look at Mary Ann. If she's still upset about what happened between Max and Winnie, she doesn't show it.

"Each team will compete in a series of events and I'll keep score. May the best team win!" says Max.

Max gets two big buckets from the pile of equipment. "The first event is an Egg Spoon Race." He gives Chloe Jennifer, Pamela, and me a

bucket filled with hard-boiled eggs that Max helped me dye red. Mary Ann, Zoe, and April get a bucket of blue eggs. Then he gives each team a spoon.

He points across the yard to two empty buckets. "The first team to successfully transport all their eggs to the bucket across the yard wins. If you drop an egg, you have to start over."

We all line up with our teams. When Max blows the whistle, we start walking one at a time with eggs on a spoon.

"Go Mallory!" yell Pamela and Chloe Jennifer as I start across the yard with an egg on a spoon. When it falls off, I pick it up and run back to the starting line.

"You can do it!" yells Chloe Jennifer.

I look at Zoe who is first on her team. Her egg dropped too and she is right back where I am. "C'mon!" Mary Ann and April yell to her.

I put my egg back on the spoon and start across the yard again. This time I walk a little more slowly and carefully. Everyone on both teams is cheering.

I get to the bucket just ahead of Zoe. "Way to go, Mallory!" Pamela and Chloe Jennifer yell as I run back with the spoon.

Both teams yell as we all take turns

taking the eggs across the yard. Pamela
is the last one up on Team Red and Mary
Ann is carrying the last egg for Team Blue.
They are side by side as they cross the yard
with their eggs. Everyone on both teams
is yelling. "C'mon, Pamela!" Chloe Jennifer
and I shout.

When she gets to the bucket a few
steps ahead of Mary Ann, we go crazy
yelling and hugging.

"Team Red is the winner of the
Egg Spoon Race," says Max. He marks
our points on the
scoreboard.

Even though Team
Blue lost, everyone on
both teams is smiling.

The next event is
a relay race, which
Team Blue wins.

Then we compete in a tug-of-war and a water-balloon toss and Team Blue wins those too.

As they cheer and hug when they win the water balloon toss, Max gives Team Red towels and a pep talk. "You better get serious if you want to win!" he says.

"I think we've got this one," Pamela says to Chloe Jennifer and me when Max announces the rules of the talkathon.

"The topic you'll be talking about is *going to the beach,*" says Max. "When I say go, the team that has the most to say wins. Ready. Set. Go!"

We all start talking about going to the beach at the same time. April and I are the last ones talking. It's close, but I have more to say on the topic than she does.

Team Red wins that event and the next one, the dance-off. We cheer and hug like crazy after both of our victories.

"It's tied at three wins for each team," announces Max.

It's pretty clear that both teams want to win, but it's also easy to see that everyone is having fun. This day is going even better than I thought it would.

"The last event, the lip sync, will decide who wins the color war at Camp Mallory," announces Max.

Each team huddles together to pick a song. Then Max gives us ten minutes to practice what we're going to do. "Time's up!" he announces. He draws a team name out of his baseball cap. "Team Red is first."

"Go Red!" Pamela, Chloe Jennifer, and I shout as we stand up to perform. Then we turn on the music. I picked the song and I feel confident as we start to perform.

But when we do, Team Blue starts laughing. Mary Ann, Zoe, and April are all rolling around on the ground cracking up. Suddenly, I feel self-conscious, like maybe this was a bad idea after all.

I click off the music. "What's so funny?" I ask.

But when I ask that question, everyone on Team Blue laughs even harder, especially Mary Ann.

"Stop laughing! I picked that song," I say. "Does somebody have a problem with it?"

"No!" says Mary Ann. "We're laughing because we're using the same song and I picked it. We had the same idea," she says with a smile.

Even though I was embarrassed just one minute ago, now I feel great. It makes me happy to know that Mary Ann and I still like some of the same things.

And it gives me another idea.

"Let's declare the color war a tie and we can all lip sync together," I say. Everyone likes that idea a lot. Except for the referee.

"What's the point of having a color war if no one wins?" asks Max.

But no one is paying attention to him. We're too busy lip syncing as a group. When we're done, I announce one more surprise. "S'mores!" I say.

My friends follow me inside to make s'mores in the oven. We make a double-decker one for Max and thank him for being a great referee. Then we take our s'mores outside and eat them in the tent.

I know graham crackers, marshmallows, and chocolate aren't the healthiest thing to eat, but everyone likes the s'mores. Even Zoe.

As I eat, I think about the talk Max and
I had. He was right. Being a good friend to
Mary Ann and focusing on my other friends
too was a good idea.

I hope Mary Ann and I get back to being
best friends like we've always been. But
more than that, I hope she'll see that if she
wants us to stay friends, she has to *act* like
a real friend.

The good news is that I had a great time

today hanging out with all my friends. I think Mary Ann did too. As I eat the last of my s'more, I lick sticky marshmallow off my finger.

It's a sweet way to end a great day.

CHAMPIONS!

Devon and I worked all week on our book report presentation.

I honestly don't think I've ever put this much work into any school project. When I told Devon that, he said he felt the same way.

Even though I wasn't too happy when we were paired up, I'm glad things worked out how they did.

Devon and I worked really well together.

MONDAY

On Monday, Devon and I met after school at my house to decide how we were going to do our presentation.

Ms. Thompson told us in class that we should think as creatively as possible when planning our reports. Then she told us that the class would vote on the best report and that there would be a prize for the winner.

"I'd like to win that prize," Devon told me.

"I would too," I told Devon.

"I have an idea," he said when we sat down to work.  "Why don't we build a puppet theater and make puppets of the main characters in the story?"

"That's an AMAZING idea!" I told Devon and we spent the rest of the afternoon working on our puppets.

TUESDAY

On Tuesday, I went over to Devon's house and we made a theater for our puppets. First, Devon drew out a plan. He started with a big box.

He cut a hole in the front of the box, then hung some curtains over the hole. I painted the front of the box to look like a mountain.

When I finished painting the box, I drew pictures of onions, since onions are a big part of the story. After I colored in my pictures, Devon helped me glue them to the bottom and sides. When we were done, our puppet theater looked amazing.

"You're going to be a good architect," I said to Devon.

"You're a great artist," said Devon. "These look like real onions."

"I love to draw," I told Devon.

I told him about the art class I took over the summer and he told me he took an acting class.

"That's cool!" I said. "I was in a school play last year."

"Our acting experience will come in handy for this project," he told me.

WEDNESDAY

On Wednesday, Devon and I put our acting skills to use.

We decided what scene we were going to act out and how we were going to act it out with our puppets. We wrote a script and when we were done we practiced.

And practiced.

And practiced.

"I think we're ready," I said after we'd practice for what felt like the 300th time.

"I think so too," said Devon.

Which we both agreed is a good thing, because presentations start tomorrow.

THURSDAY

On Thursday, Devon and I actually did NOTHING.

That's because only half the class got to give their presentations that day, and Devon and I were not in that half. Some of the presentations were only OK, but some were really good, like the musical interpretation Mary Ann and Zoe did about the book *Wonder,* and the board game that Pete and Jackson made about *Because of Winn Dixie.*

"I can't believe we have to wait until tomorrow," Devon said to me when class was over.

"Watching the other presentations made me nervous," I told him.

Now it's Friday and I'm more nervous today than I was yesterday. I can hardly eat the eggs Mom made for breakfast. Before I leave the house, I send a text.

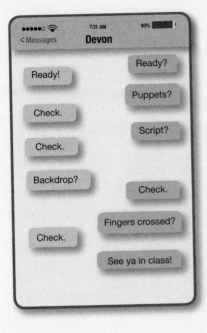

When Ms. Thompson starts class, the few bites of eggs I ate feel like they're doing flip-flops in my stomach.

"We're going to do great," Devon whispers to me when the first team goes up to the front of the class to start their presentation. I think he can tell I'm nervous and is trying to make me feel better.

We sit through three presentations before Ms. Thompson calls on us.

When it's our turn, Devon and I walk to the front of the class and set up the theater we made. We crouch down behind it so the class can't see us and we put our puppets on our hands.

"Ready?" whispers Devon.

"Ready!" I whisper back.

Then we start our show. We hold up our puppets so the class can see them and we go through our script. Line by line, we act out the scene where Stanley and Zero climb the mountain. We do it just like we practiced it, except for some reason, it sounds even better than it did when we rehearsed it at Devon's house.

When we're done, we stand up and take a bow and the whole class claps.

"That was fabulous," says Ms. Thompson. "What a creative way to tell the story." I think the class must agree with Ms. Thompson, because they keep clapping.

When the applause dies down, Ms. Thompson calls on the next pair of presenters.

There's one more set after that and then Ms. Thompson says it's time to vote.

She passes around sheets of paper with all the pairs of presenters listed with the name of their books. "I'd like everyone to put a check mark by the pair whose presentation you enjoyed the most. I'll tally up the results and announce a winner."

Devon and I glance at each other. We both want to win. Our report was good, but there were a lot of good reports. It's hard to know who will win. Ms. Thompson collects the ballots, and then sits down at her desk to see who won.

I cross my toes and look at Devon.

Ms. Thompson stands up to announce the winner. "Congratulations Mallory and Devon. You're the winners of the book-report contest."

Devon and I grin at each other as Ms.

Thompson gives us each a trophy. Then we get gift cards to The Fern Falls Scoop. It's the best ice-cream place in town.

Everyone crowds around us to see our trophies.

"Great job!" says Pete.

Jackson high-fives us.

"Congratulations!" says Zoe. "That was amazing."

"Awesome!" says Mary Ann.

I look at her and smile. Even though she and Zoe didn't win, they did a really good job. But I can tell she's happy for me and it makes me feel good.

I feel even better when Ms. Thompson comes over to me when class ends. "Mallory, I'm very proud of you," she says. "I see how hard you're working and I couldn't be any more delighted."

"Thanks," I tell Ms. Thompson.

I think about the letter I wrote to her at the beginning of the year. I wrote that I wanted fifth grade to be the best year ever. It didn't start out that way. I got off on the wrong foot with Ms. Thompson. Mary Ann became close friends with Zoe. And I got stuck with a book report partner I thought I didn't want.

But things are getting better.

My teacher sees that I'm a good student. Mary Ann and I are still friends. Maybe not the way we've always been, but things are getting better. And Devon turned out to be the best book-report partner ever!

I don't know what the rest of fifth grade will be like. I guess I'll have to take things one day at a time. Hopefully, more good things are in store for me.

There's one really good thing I know for sure is in store for me: ice cream!

FAMILY FUN

Dinner is ready! NOW!

I pick my phone
up off my desk
and look at it.
When I do, I'm
surprised. I have a
text from Mom!
I smile as
I scoop up
Cheeseburger and
skip down the hall

from my room to the kitchen. I'm happy for several reasons.

One. Ever since I invited everyone over to my house for color war, things have been better with Mary Ann. I could tell she had fun doing something that day with Zoe and me and our other friends too, and she was happy for me today when Devon and I won the book-report contest.

Two. Max has been a great brother lately. He's been really extra nice. I don't know if it has anything to do with him going out with Sam, but I know I like it!

Three. Devon and I won the book-report contest! We put a lot of work into it, so I'm not surprised we did well. But it's nice that our classmates voted for us, and we didn't win just because Ms. Thompson thought we did a good job.

Four. It smells like we're having spaghetti and meatballs, which is my all-time favorite dinner!

"This looks great!" I say to Mom as I sit down. Max and Dad are already at the table. I reach for the pasta bowl, but Max beats me to it.

"Hey! What happened to ladies first?" I ask.

"I don't see any ladies here," says Max helping himself to a huge plate of noodles and sauce and meatballs.

"Max!" both my parents say his name at the same time.

"Sorry," he says like he hadn't meant to offend anyone. Then, he looks at me and grins. I grin back. I know he was just teasing me and I don't mind it.

I fill my plate and then take a big bite. "Mmm!" I say.

Then I tell my family about the presentation Devon and I did today, "I wish you could have seen it," I say. My family knows how hard Devon and I worked on our book report all week, and

they saw the trophy I brought home this afternoon, but they all listen while I fill them in on the details.

"When Ms. Thompson announced we'd won, she said that Devon's architectural and acting skills plus my art skills resulted in a winning equation!"

"Mallory, I'm so proud of you!" says Dad. "This calls for a celebration. How about we all put on our pajamas after dinner and have family movie night?"

Max looks at me and rolls his eyes. I can tell he doesn't think family movie night sounds like a fun way to celebrate and neither do I. It's hard to all agree on a movie.

"I have a better idea," I say. I stand up and pull the gift card Ms. Thompson gave me out of my back pocket. I hold it up so everyone can see what I won. "Why don't we go for ice cream after dinner?"

"That's a great idea!" says Max.

"I'm in," says Mom.

"Sounds like a plan," says Dad.

Max and I help Mom clean up, and then we pile into the car. "Hey, Mal," says Dad as he pulls out of the driveway. "I'm proud of you. You worked hard and it paid off."

"I'm proud of you too," says Max.

I can't help it, but I start laughing. It just doesn't sound like something Max would say. "You're just happy we get to go for ice cream," I tell him.

Max grins. "Busted."

When we get to the ice cream parlor, Dad says I get to order first. I look at the menu board. It's hard to choose. There are so many flavors of ice cream and different types of sundaes. While I'm trying to figure out what I want, I can't help but think that life is kind of like picking ice cream.

There are lots of choices. I made a good one when I decided to invite all my friends over for color war. I made another good one when Devon and I decided to

The FERN FALLS FREEZE *

CELEBRATION SUNDAE 6⁹⁵
MALTS & SHAKES 3⁹⁵
BANANA SPLIT 4⁹⁵
SUNDAE 3⁹⁵
CUP OR CONE 2⁹⁵

make the puppet theater for our book-report project.

As I look at the menu board, I know I'm about to make another good choice. "We'll have the celebration sundae," I say to the guy working behind the counter. "Is it OK if we all split it?" I ask Mom and Dad and Max.

Mom and Dad look at each other and nod like they hadn't expected me to order that, but they like the idea. Max looks like he approves too. Why wouldn't he?

Four scoops, four toppings, bananas, nuts, whipped cream, and a cherry on top with the people who matter most.

What could be better than that?

DOS AND DON'TS

Going from fourth to fifth grade is a big switch. Trust me, I know. I've learned a lot since I started school (and I'm not just talking about the stuff in my textbooks).

Here are my top ten tips to help you start a new school year off right. And the good news is that these tips should work no matter what grade you're in!

Mallory McDonald's Top 10 Tips for a Great School Year!

DOS

1. DO respect your teacher's privacy. (Especially if she's new!) Actually, this advice applies to old teachers too!

2. DO follow the rules. (About phones and everything else!)

3. DO put a lot of work into your school projects. (Especially book reports!) And don't be afraid to try something creative!

4. DO try to be a good friend—and always be ready to make new friends too.

5. DO take it one day at a time. If things don't seem good at first, don't worry. You never know what tomorrow will bring!

DON'TS

6. DON'T worry if your friends start doing new things. (Like drinking smoothies!) And hey, maybe even give those things a try. You might like them!

7. DON'T worry if your old friends make some new friends. Just keep being a good friend and try to focus on some of your other friends.

8. DON'T worry if you get stuck working on a project with a partner you don't want. You might end up being really glad you did!

9. DON'T freak out if you get into trouble with your teacher. Teachers get that kids make mistakes. Just try to show your teacher that you're working hard.

10. DON'T do something just because someone else tells you to (like ask your teacher a personal question).

If you follow these tips, I'm pretty sure (actually, totally sure) you'll have a great year!

Good luck! I hope you have the best school year ever!

RECIPES

Try this recipe for Baked S'mores that my friends and I made. They're simple to make and even simpler to eat! I know your friends will love them just as much as mine did. Get an adult's OK to use the oven!

Baked S'mores
(Serves 4)

Ingredients
4 regular-sized graham crackers
    (broken into halves)
2 milk-chocolate
    bars (broken
    into halves)
4 marshmallows

Directions

1. Preheat the oven to 400 degrees F.
2. Lay graham crackers on a cookie sheet. Top half of the graham crackers with chocolate bars. Place marshmallows on remaining graham crackers.
3. Bake until the marshmallows are puffed and golden brown, about 1-3 minutes. Remove from the oven and press one chocolate-covered graham cracker with one marshmallow-covered graham cracker to make a sandwich. Eat while warm and enjoy every bite!

If you want to make a healthier treat, try this recipe!

Strawberry-Banana Smoothies
(Serves 4)

Ingredients
2 1/2 cups of frozen strawberries
4 ripe bananas
1 1/2 cups of milk (you can use soy,
    almond, or rice milk—or even
    apple juice if you like your
    smoothies extra sweet!)
1 cup of ice

Directions

1. Put all ingredients into a blender and mix on low power until well blended.
2. Pour into tall glasses, stick in a straw (I like cute, colorful ones best), and enjoy!

Darby Creek
A division of Lerner Publishing Group, Inc.
241 First Avenue North
Minneapolis, MN 55401 USA

For reading levels and more information, look up this title at
www.lernerbooks.com.

Cover background: © iStockphoto.com/RusN

Main body text set in LumarcLL 14/20. Typeface provided by Linotype.

Library of Congress Cataloging-in-Publication Data

Names: Friedman, Laurie B., 1964– author. | Kalis, Jennifer, illustrator.
Title: High five mallory! by Laurie Friedman ; illustrations by Jennifer Kalis.
Description: minneapolis : Darby Creek, [2016] | Series: mallory ; #25 |
    Summary: mallory starts fifth grade and has to adjust to a new teacher,
    a tough school project, and trouble with her best friend that involves her
    brother max.
Identifiers: LCCN 2015035322| ISBN 9781467750301 (lb : alk. paper) |
    ISBN 9781512408980 (eb pdf)
Subjects: | CYAC: Schools—Fiction. | Friendship—Fiction. | Brothers and
    sisters—Fiction.
Classification: LCC PZ7.F89773 Hi 2016 | DDC [Fic]—dc23

LC record available at http://lccn.loc.gov/2015035322

Manufactured in the United States of America
1 — BP — 7/15/16

SUSTAINABLE FORESTRY INITIATIVE

Certified Chain of Custody
Promoting Sustainable Forestry
www.sfiprogram.org
SFI-01268

SFI label applies to the text stock